GRIEF
IS THE THING
WITH FEATHERS

GRIEF
IS THE THING
WITH FEATHERS

MAX PORTER

FABER & FABER

GRIEF
IS THE THING
WITH FEATHERS

MAX PORTER

FABER & FABER

First published in 2015
by Faber & Faber Ltd
Bloomsbury House
74–77 Great Russell Street
London WC1B 3DA

Typeset by Faber & Faber Ltd
Printed in the UK by CPI Group (UK) Ltd, Croydon, CR0 4YY

The right of Max Porter to be identified as author of this work
has been asserted in accordance with Section 77 of the Copyright,
Designs and Patents Act 1988

'That Love is all there is' from *The Poems of Emily Dickinson: Variorum
Edition*, edited by Ralph W. Franklin, Cambridge, Mass.: The Belknap
Press of Harvard University Press, Copyright © 1998 by the President and
Fellows of Harvard College. Copyright © 1951, 1955, 1979, 1983 by the
President and Fellows of Harvard College.

A CIP record for this book
is available from the British Library

ISBN 978-0-571-32376-0

10 9 8 7 6

For Roly

That Love is all there is, [CROW]
Is all we know of Love; [CROW]
It is enough, the freight should be [CROW]
Proportioned to the groove. [CROW]

Emily Dickinson

PART ONE A LICK OF NIGHT

BOYS

There's a feather on my pillow.

Pillows are made of feathers, go to sleep.

It's a big, black feather.

Come and sleep in my bed.

There's a feather on your pillow too.

Let's leave the feathers where they are and sleep on the floor.

DAD

Four or five days after she died, I sat alone in the living room wondering what to do. Shuffling around, waiting for shock to give way, waiting for any kind of structured feeling to emerge from the organisational fakery of my days. I felt hung-empty. The children were asleep. I drank. I smoked roll-ups out of the window. I felt that perhaps the main result of her being gone would be that I would permanently become this organiser, this list-making trader in clichés of gratitude, machine-like architect of routines for small children with no Mum. Grief felt fourth-dimensional, abstract, faintly familiar. I was cold.

The friends and family who had been hanging around being kind had gone home to their own lives. When the children went to bed the flat had no meaning, nothing moved.

The doorbell rang and I braced myself for more kindness. Another lasagne, some books, a cuddle, some little potted ready-meals for the boys. Of course, I was becoming expert in the behaviour of orbiting grievers. Being at the epicentre grants a curiously anthropological awareness of everybody else; the overwhelmeds, the affectedly lackadaisicals, the nothing so fars, the overstayers, the new best friends of hers, of mine, of the boys. The people I still have no fucking idea who they were. I felt like Earth in that extraordinary picture of the planet surrounded by a thick belt of space junk. I felt it would be years before the knotted-string dream of other people's performances of woe for my dead wife would thin enough for me to see any black space again, and of course – needless to say – thoughts of this kind made me feel guilty. But, I thought, in support of myself, everything has changed, and she is gone and I can think what I like. She would approve, because we were always over-analytical, cynical, probably disloyal, puzzled. Dinner party post-mortem bitches with kind intentions. Hypocrites. Friends.

The bell rang again.

I climbed down the carpeted stairs into the chilly hallway and opened the front door.

There were no streetlights, bins or paving stones. No shape or light, no form at all, just a stench.

There was a crack and a whoosh and I was smacked back, winded, onto the doorstep. The hallway was pitch black and freezing cold and I thought, 'What kind of world is it that I would be robbed in my home tonight?' And then I thought, 'Frankly, what does it matter?' I thought, 'Please don't wake the boys, they need their sleep. I will give you every penny I own just as long as you don't wake the boys.'

I opened my eyes and it was still dark and everything was crackling, rustling.

Feathers.

There was a rich smell of decay, a sweet furry stink of just-beyond-edible food, and moss, and leather, and yeast.

Feathers between my fingers, in my eyes, in my mouth, beneath me a feathery hammock lifting me up a foot above the tiled floor.

One shiny jet-black eye as big as my face, blinking slowly, in a leathery wrinkled socket, bulging out from a football-sized testicle.

SHHHHHHHHHHHHH.

                                        shhhhhhhh.

And this is what he said:

I won't leave until you don't need me any more.

                                Put me down, I said.

Not until you say hello.

        Put. Me. Down, I croaked, and my piss warmed the
                                cradle of his wing.

You're frightened. Just say hello.

                                        Hello.

Say it properly.

I lay back, resigned, and wished my wife wasn't dead. I wished I wasn't lying terrified in a giant bird embrace in my hallway. I wished I hadn't been obsessing about this thing just when the greatest tragedy of my life occurred. These were factual yearnings. It was bitterly wonderful. I had some clarity.

Hello Crow, I said. Good to finally meet you.

*

And he was gone.

For the first time in days I slept. I dreamt of afternoons in the forest.

CROW

Very romantic, how we first met. Badly behaved. Trip
trap. Two-bed upstairs flat, spit-level, slight barbed-
error, snuck in easy through the wall and up the attic
bedroom to see those cotton boys silently sleeping,
intoxicating hum of innocent children, lint, flack,
gack-pack-nack, the whole place was heavy mourning,
every surface dead Mum, every crayon, tractor, coat,
welly, covered in a film of grief. Down the dead Mum
stairs, plinkety plink curled claws whisper, down to
Daddy's recently Mum-and-Dad's bedroom. I was
Herne the hunter hornless, funt. Munt. Here he is.
Out. Drunk-for white. I bent down over him and
smelt his breath. Notes of rotten hedge, bluebottles.
I prised open his mouth and counted bones, snacked
a little on his un-brushed teeth, flossed him, crowly
tossed his tongue hither, thither, I lifted the duvet.
I Eskimo kissed him. I butterfly kissed him. I flat-
flutter Jenny Wren kissed him. His lint (toe-jam-rint)
fuck-sacks sad and cosy, sagging, gently rising, then
down, rising, then down, rising, then down, I was
praying the breathing and the epidermis whispered
'flesh, aah, flesh, aah, flesh, aah', and it was beautiful
for me, rising (just like me) then down (just like me)
pan-shaped (just like me) it was any wonder the facts
of my arrival under his sheets didn't lift him, stench,

rot-yot-kot, wake up human (BIRD FEATHERS UP YER CRACK, DOWN YER COCK-EYE, IN YER MOUTH) but he slept and the bedroom was a mausoleum. He was an accidental remnant and I knew this was the best gig, a real bit of fun. I put my claw on his eyeball and weighed up gouging it out for fun or mercy. I plucked one jet feather from my hood and left it on his forehead, for, his, head.

For a souvenir, for a warning, for a lick of night in the morning.

For a little break in the mourning.
I will give you something to think about, I whispered. He woke up and didn't see me against the blackness of his trauma.

ghoeeeze, he clacked.

ghoeeeze.

DAD

Today I got back to work.

I managed half an hour then doodled.

I drew a picture of the funeral. Everybody had crow
faces, except for the boys.

CROW

Look at that, look, did I or did I not, oi, look, stab it.
Good book, funny bodies, open door, slam door, spit
this, lick that, lift, oi, look, stop it.

Tender opportunity. Never mind, every evening,
crack of dawn, all change, all meat this, all meat that,
separate the reek. Did I or did I not, ooh, tarmac
macadam. Edible, sticky, bad camouflage.

Strap me to the mast or I'll bang her until my
mathematics poke out her sorry, sorry, sorry, look! A
severed hand, bramble, box of swans, box of stories,
piss-arc, better off, must stop shaking, must stay still,
mast stay still.

Oi, look, trust me. Did I or did I not faithfully deliver St Vincent to Lisbon. Safe trip, a bit of liver, sniff, sniff, fabric softener, leather, railings melted for bombs, bullets. Did I or did I not carry the hag across the river. Shit not, did not. Sing song blackbird automatic fuck-you-yellow, nasty, pretty boy, joke, creak, joke, crech, joke. Patience.

I could've bent him backwards over a chair and drip-fed him sour bulletins of the true one-hour dying of his wife. OTHER BIRDS WOULD HAVE, there's no goody baddy in the kingdom. Better get cracking.

I believe in the therapeutic method.

BOYS

We were small boys with remote-control cars and ink-stamp sets and we knew something was up. We knew we weren't getting straight answers when we asked 'where is Mum?' and we knew, even before we were taken to our room and told to sit on the bed, either side of Dad, that something was changed. We guessed and understood that this was a new life and Dad was a different type of Dad now and we were different boys, we were brave new boys without a Mum. So when he told us what had happened I don't know what my brother was thinking but I was thinking this:

Where are the fire engines? Where is the noise and clamour of an event like this? Where are the strangers going out of their way to help, screaming, flinging bits of emergency glow-in-the-dark equipment at us to try and settle us and save us?

There should be men in helmets speaking
a new and dramatic language of crisis.
There should be horrible levels of noise,
completely foreign and inappropriate for
our cosy London flat.

There were no crowds and no uniformed
strangers and there was no new language
of crisis. We stayed in our PJs and people
visited and gave us stuff.

Holiday and school became the same.

CROW

In other versions I am a doctor or a ghost. Perfect
devices: doctors, ghosts and crows. We can do things
other characters can't, like eat sorrow, un-birth secrets
and have theatrical battles with language and God. I
was friend, excuse, deus ex machina, joke, symptom,
figment, spectre, crutch, toy, phantom, gag, analyst
and babysitter.

I was, after all, 'the central bird . . . at every extreme'.
I'm a template. I know that, he knows that. A myth to
be slipped in. Slip up into.

Inevitably I have to defend my position, because my
position is sentimental. You don't know your origin
tales, your biological truth (accident), your deaths
(mosquito bites, mostly), your lives (denial, cheerfully).
I am reluctant to discuss absurdity with any of you,
who have persecuted us since time began. What good is
a crow to a pack of grieving humans? A huddle.
A throb.
     A sore.
        A plug.
           A gape.
              A load.
A gap.

So, yes. I do eat baby rabbits, plunder nests, swallow filth, cheat death, mock the starving homeless, misdirect, misinform. Oi, stab it! A bloody load of time wasted.

But I care, deeply. I find humans dull except in grief. There are very few in health, disaster, famine, atrocity, splendour or normality that interest me (interest ME!) but the motherless children do. Motherless children are pure crow. For a sentimental bird it is ripe, rich and delicious to raid such a nest.

DAD

I've drawn her unpicked, ribs splayed stretched like a xylophone with the dead birds playing tunes on her bones.

CROW

I've written hundreds of memoirs. It's necessary for
big names like me. I believe it is called the imperative.

Once upon a time there was a blood wedding, and the
crow son was angry that his mother was marrying
again. So he flew away. He flew to find his father
but all he found was carrion. He made friends with
farmers (he delivered other birds to their guns),
scientists (he performed tricks with tools that not
even chimps could perform), and a poet or two. He
thought, on several occasions, that he had found
his Daddy's bones, and he wept and screamed at the
hateful Goshawks 'here are the grey bones of my
hooded Papa', but every time when he looked again
it was some other corvid's corpse. So, tired of the
fable lifestyle, sick of his omen celebrity, he hopped
and flew and dragged himself home. The wedding
party was still in full swing and the ancient grey crow
rutting with his mother in the pile of trash at the foot
of the stairs was none other than his father. The crow
son screamed his hurt and confusion at his writhing
parents. His father laughed. KONK. KONK. KONK.
You've lived a long time and been a crow through and
through, but you still can't take a joke.

DAD

Soft.

     Slight.

          Like light, like a child's foot talcum-dusted and kissed, like stroke-reversing suede, like dust, like pins and needles, like a promise, like a curse, like seeds, like everything grained, plaited, linked, or numbered, like everything nature-made and violent and quiet.

It is all completely missing. Nothing patient now.

BOYS

My brother and I discovered a guppy fish in a
rock pool somewhere. We set about trying to
kill it. First we flung shingle into the pool but
the fish was fast. Then we tried large rocks and
boulders, but the fish would hide in the corners
beneath small crevices, or dart away. We were
human boys and the fish was just a fish, so
we devised a way to kill it. We filled the pool
with stones, blocking and damming the guppy
into a smaller and smaller area. Soon it circled
slowly and sadly in the tiny prison-pool and
we selected a perfectly sized stone. My brother
slammed it down over-arm and it popped and
splashed, rock on rock in water and delightedly
we lifted it out. Sure enough the fish was dead.
All the fun was sucked across the wide empty
beach. I felt sick and my brother swore. He
suggested flinging the lifeless guppy into the
sea but I couldn't bring myself to touch it so
we sprinted back across the beach and Dad
didn't look up from his book but said 'you've
done something bad I can tell'.

DAD

We will never fight again, our lovely, quick, template-ready arguments. Our delicate cross-stitch of bickers.

The house becomes a physical encyclopedia of no-longer hers, which shocks and shocks and is the principal difference between our house and a house where illness has worked away. Ill people, in their last day on Earth, do not leave notes stuck to bottles of red wine saying 'OH NO YOU DON'T COCK-CHEEK'. She was not busy dying, and there is no detritus of care, she was simply busy living, and then she was gone.

She won't ever use (make-up, turmeric, hairbrush, thesaurus).

She will never finish (Patricia Highsmith novel, peanut butter, lip balm).

And I will never shop for green Virago Classics for her birthday.

I will stop finding her hairs.

I will stop hearing her breathing.

BOYS

We found a fish in a pool and tried to kill
it but the pool was too big and the fish was
too quick so we dammed it and smashed it.
Later on, for ages, my brother did pictures
of the pool, of the fish, of us. Diagrams
explaining our choices. My brother always
uses diagrams to explain our choices, but
they aren't scientific, they're scrappy. My
brother likes to do scrappy badly drawn
diagrams even though he can actually
draw pretty well.

CROW

Head down, tot-along, looking.
Head down, hop-down, totter.
Look up. 'LOUD, HARD AND INDIGNANT
    KRAAH NOTES' (*Collins Guide to Birds*, p. 45).
Head down, bottle-top, potter.
Head down, mop-a-lot, hopper.
He could learn a lot from me.
That's why I'm here.

DAD

There is a fascinating constant exchange between
Crow's natural self and his civilised self, between
the scavenger and the philosopher, the goddess of
complete being and the black stain, between Crow
and his birdness. It seems to me to be the self-same
exchange between mourning and living, then and
now. I could learn a lot from him.

BOYS

Dad has gone. Crow is in the bathroom,
where he often is because he likes the
acoustics. We are crouched by the closed
door listening. He is speaking very slowly,
very clearly. He sounds old-fashioned, like
Dad's vinyl recording of Dylan Thomas.
He says SUDDEN. He says TRAUMA. He
says Induced . . . he coughs and spits and
tries again, INDUCED. He says SUDDEN
TRAUMA INDUCED ALTERATION OF
THE ALERT STATE.

Dad comes back. Crow changes his tune.

CROW

Gormin'ere, worrying horrid. Hello elair, krip krap
krip krap who's that lazurusting beans of my cut-
out? Let me buck flap snutch clat tapa one tapa
two, motherless children in my trap, in my apse, in
separate stocks for boiling, Enunciate it, rolling and
turning it, sadget lips and burning it. Ooh, pressure!
Must rehearse, must cuss less. The nobility of nature,
haha krah haha krap haha, better not.

(I do this, perform some unbound crow stuff, for
him. I think he thinks he's a little bit Stonehenge
shamanic, hearing the bird spirit. Fine by me,
whatever gets him through.)

Megalith!

PART TWO DEFENCE OF THE NEST

DAD

Fourteen months to finish the book for Parenthesis Press: *Ted Hughes'* Crow *on the Couch: A Wild Analysis.*

I have a scruffy Manchester-based publisher who sends me encouraging notes and says he would understand if it was too much, now, to write a book. We are agreed the book will reflect the subject. It will hop about a bit. Parenthesis hope my book might appeal to everyone sick of Ted & Sylvia archaeology. It's not about them, we agree. We neglect to discuss what it should be about.

Every time I sit down and look at my notes Crow appears in my office. Sometimes slouched on the floor, resting on one wing ('Look! I'm the Venus of Corvino!'), sometimes patiently perched on my shoulder advising me ('Is that fair on Baskin, really?'). Most of the time he is happy to sit curled

in the armchair quietly reading, wheezing. He flicks
through picture books and poetry collections, tutting
and sighing. He has no time for novels. He only picks
up history books to label great men fuckwits or curse
the church. He enjoys memoirs and was delighted
to discover the book about a Scottish woman who
adopted a rook.

CROW

Once upon a time there was a babysitting bird,
let's call him Crow. He had read too many Russian
fairy tales (lazy boy burn, Baba Yaga howl, decent
Prince win), but was nevertheless an authorised
and accredited caregiver, much admired by London
parents, much in demand of a Friday night. On his
newsagent advert it was written:

'Nappy Valley: And Beyond!'

The telly went off and Crow suggested a game.
'You two boys', he said, 'must each build – here on the
floor – a model of your Mother. Just as you remember
her! And whichever of you builds the best model will

win. Not the most realistic, but the best, the truest. The prize is this . . .' said the Crow, stroking their shampooed hair . . . 'the best model I will bring to life, a living mother to tuck you up in bed.'

And so the boys set to it.

The one son went for drawing, furiously concentrating like a little waist-high fresco painter scrabbling hands and knees on the scaffold. Thirty-seven taped-together sheets of A4 paper and the full rainbow of crayons, pencils and pens, his front teeth biting down on his lower lip. Heavy nasal sighing as he adjusted the eyes, scrapped them, started again, working his way down, happy with the hands, happy with the legs.

The second son went for assemblage, a model of the woman made from cutlery, ribbons, stationery, toys, buttons and books, manically adjusting – leaping up, lying down – like a mechanic in the pits. Clicking and tutting as he worked his way around the mosaic mum, happy with the face, happy with the height. And, 'Stop!' said the Crow.

'They are both extraordinary,' he said, admiring their work, 'you've got her smile, you've captured her posture, her shoulders were hunched to that exact degree!'

And the boys couldn't wait to find out who had won; 'Which one?! Which Mum?!', but Crow started hopping, avoiding their gaze, suppressing a giggle and turning away.

'Crow, which one of these fake mums has won us a real one?'

And Crow was quiet, laughing no more.

'Crow, don't be funny, let's have our real Mummy.' And Crow started crying.

And the boys cooked Crow in a very hot oven until he was nothing but cells.

This is Crow's bad dream.

BOYS

Yes? she said, before she was dead.
We don't want baths, our bums are clean!
We both had a bath last night.
Fine, she said. Straight to bed for stories.

Yes? she said, before she was dead.
We don't want baths, our bums are clean!
We both had a bath last night.
Well, she said, no bath, no stories.

You decide.

DAD

*We will fill this house with toys and books and wail
like playgroup left-behinds.*

I refused to lose a wife and gain chores, so I accepted
help. My brother was incredible, *give me food, let
me shout,* with the boys, with the bank, with the
post office, the school, the doctors and our folks. Her
parents were kind, with the service, with the money,
with their people, *give me space, give me time, give
me sense of her, let me apologise, let me find a path
outside simple fury.* Her friends, our families, with
the news and the details, and her stuff, doing her
proud, doing it right, teasing out a route and tailoring
it to us, and not a cliché in sight.

BOYS

Not long after, our Gran was dying.
We were told we could go up, so we went
up. The carpet was deep and soft and we
were barefoot. She had an oxygen tank
on wheels. We went either side of the bed
and each held a hand. The hand I held was
crinkled and soft and amazingly warm.
She said she had some things to tell us if
we were ready to hear them. We said we
were ready. Born ready Gran, my brother
said, which I thought was inappropriate,
but she said 'Yes, born ready darling'.

She told us that men were rarely truly
kind, but they were often funny, which
is better. 'You would do well to prepare
yourselves for disappointment' she said,
'in your dealings with men. Women are on
the whole much stronger, usually cleverer'
she said, 'but less funny, which is a shame.
Have babies, if you can' she said 'because
you'll be good at it. Help yourselves to

anything you find in this house. I want to give you everything I have because you are the most precious and beautiful boys. You remind me of everything I have ever been interested in' she said.

'Do you hate seeing me wheeze?'

No, we said, it's fine.

'Help yourself to the cigarettes in the kitchen drawers' she said, 'and one day you too will wheeze like me. The daisies on my grave will puff and wheeze, you mark my words.'

We stayed while she slept and a tall woman in a tight white uniform changed her covers.

DAD

By the side of the road was a young dead fox, eyes
open, stuck frozen to the grass, looking more still-
born than road-killed.

I could cycle it to Heptonstall or bring it defrosting to
the kitchen and set it down for my sons to see.
I am obsessed.

I remember the night I got home and told her I'd
finished the book proposal, and she said, 'God help us
all,' and we drank Prosecco and she said I could have
my birthday present early. It was the plastic crow.
We made love and I kissed her shoulder blades and
reminded her of the story of my parents lying to me
about children growing wings and she said, 'My body
is not bird-like.'

We were smack bang in the middle, years from the
finish, taking nothing for granted.

I want to be there again. Again, and again. I want to
be held, I wanted to hold. It was the plastic crow.

We made love. The wing story. My body is not bird-
like.
Again.

      The wings.

              The love.

                    Bird-like.

Again. I beg everything again.

BOYS

We used to play a game called Sonic
Boom. We would fly as fast as we could
through the pine forest like bullets
through a crowd and we would compete to
turn at the very last moment before a tree.
We would fly as fast as we could through
the pine forest and then flip, roll sideways
millimetres from the tree, shrieking Sonic
BOOM as we reeled off. One day I taunted
my brother. I dared him to ricochet off
the tree like a bullet glancing off a fleeing
shoulder. I went first and I flew hard and
true straight towards a tree and Sonic
BOOM at the final moment swerved
and my wing slapped the trunk, whap,
and I barrelled off into the forest (like a
bullet glancing off a fleeing shoulder).
My brother flew too low and too fast and
never turned, whap, a sharpened branch
pierced him right through the neck and he
hung there crawking 'sonic. sonic. sonic.'
This is only partially true.

DAD

They played at birds, they played at lions. They went
through phases: dinosaurs, trucks, Thundercats, kung
fu, lying, sport.

There was very little division between their
imaginary and real worlds, and people talked of coping
mechanisms and normal childhood and time. Many
people said 'You need time', when what we needed
was washing powder, nit shampoo, football stickers,
batteries, bows, arrows, bows, arrows.

There was very little division between my imaginary
and real worlds, and people talked of sensible
workloads and recovery periods and healthy
obsessions. Many people said 'You need time',
when what I needed was Shakespeare, Ibn 'Arabi,
Shostakovich, Howlin' Wolf.

I remember they left their tea unfinished and I picked
at half-eaten fish fingers, cold peas and coagulated
ketchup.

I remember I said, 'I'm throwing every single toy in the bin!' and they giggled.

I remember being scared that something must, surely, go wrong, if we were this happy, her and me, in the early days, when our love was settling into the shape of our lives like cake mixture reaching the corners of the tin as it swells and bakes.

I remember my first date, aged fifteen, with a girl called Hilary Gidding. A coin fell down the back of the cinema seats and we both slipped our hands into the tight fuzzy gap of the chairs past popcorn kernels and sticky ticket stubs and our hands met, stroking the carpet feeling for the coin, and it was electric. The wrist being clamped by upholstery, the darkness, the accident, the lovely dirt of public spaces.

BOYS

Dad and Crow were fighting in the
living room. Door closed. There was a
low droning cawera skraa, caw, cawera
skraa and Dad saying Stop it, Stop it,
caw, craw, and hocking, retching, spitting,
bad language, cronks, barks, sobs, a weird
gamelan jam of broken father sounds and
violent bird calls, thumps and shrieks and
twinging rips.

Crow emerged, ruffled, wide-eyed. He
gently closed the door behind him and
joined us at the kitchen table.

We coloured in zoo pictures with our felt-
tipped pens and Crow went over the lines.

DAD

I remember her pushing when they told her to push
and the Jamaican midwife saying, 'Push gyal, push
gyal.' She said, 'I don't want to poo,' and I laughed
and said, 'Too late.' Then there was son one, covered
in strange smelly cream, hungry and tiny.

I remember her pushing when they told her to push
and the Scottish midwife saying, 'Blimey, here comes
a head.' She said, 'It hurts, fuck, fuck-fuck it hurts,'
and we were crying and there was son two, purple,
howling and bendy.

She is Mrs Laocoön, standing on the beach with her
arms crossed, saying, 'Look at those bloody boys,'
and we are fifty feet out to sea being chewed apart by
sadness.

BOYS

Some of the time we tell the truth. It's our
way of being nice to Dad.

DAD

Introduction: Crow's Bad Dream I miss my wife
Ch. 1. ~~Magical Dangers~~ I miss my wife
Ch. 2. ~~Reign of Silence~~ I miss my wife
Ch. 3. ~~Unkillable Trickster~~ I miss my wife
Ch. 4. ~~Aphrodisiac Disaster~~ I miss my wife
Ch. 5. ~~Tragic Comedy~~ I miss my wife
Ch. 6. ~~The Baby (God) in the Lake~~ I miss my wife
Ch. 7. ~~The Song~~ I miss my wife
Conclusion: Recovery and Growth I miss my wife

CROW

Once upon a time there were two big men who were brothers with one another. They were in brother with each other.

The soles of the bigger brother's boots were worn through in patches. Half a mile out of the village on Windmill Hill his socks were damp and squelching and he mentioned turning back for better boots but the smaller brother kept walking.

'The only other pair of boots is my old pair and they would be too small for you.'
　'True.'
　'My spare boots are better than your only boots.'

They trudged up the steep hill mounting thin banks of chalk like swimmers moving out past breaking waves and at the top they paused to gaze down at the village sitting neatly in the cupped hand of the valley.

'You will struggle in shit boots brother. At some point we might walk on sharp flints or need to tread down thorny branches.'
　'I imagine at some point we might.'
　'Then you will struggle is all I'm saying.'

The smaller brother hocked and spat a ball of ochre phlegm at the gate of the windmill and cursed the owner. The bigger brother laughed.

They walked fast down through the pollard wood that clad the far side of Windmill Hill. A roof of luminous patchwork was suspended above them and the dark floor was stabbed all over with light.

A red deer bolted from a holly bush and the bigger brother whispered, 'Hello friend.'

The other brother made a gun with his hand and shrieked 'KABOOM' and a startled pheasant barrelled upwards into the neon green with a chuckle.

Comprehension Questions:

- Do you think the brothers in this excerpt are realistic?
- Does the rural setting of the story change the way you engage with the characters?
- If the boots are a metaphor for the ability to cope with grief, who do you think has died?
- Write the next paragraph of the story, focusing on the themes of man versus nature, boots, brothers, and the Russian revolution.

BOYS

She was beaten to death, I once told some
   boys at a party.
Oh shit mate, they said.
I lie about how you died, I whispered to
   Mum.
I would do the same, she whispered back.

DAD

I remember her pretending to like watching award
ceremonies more than she actually did because it
surprised me, but then I let her know that such-and-
such award ceremony was on and we would have to
sit through it. Let's go to bed, she said, we don't really
know who any of these people are.

Winners, I said. Every stinking ugly vacuous cunt-
faced last one of them.

And off we went to bed.

Some days I realise I've been forgetting basic things,
so I run upstairs, or downstairs, or wherever they
are and I say, 'You must know that your Mum was
the funniest, most excellent person. She was my
best friend. She was so sarcastic and affectionate . . .'
and then I run out of steam because it feels so crass
and lazy, and they nod and say, 'We know, Dad, we
remember.'

'She would call me sentimental.'

'You are sentimental.'

They offer me a space on the sofa next to them
and the pain of them being so naturally kind is like
appendicitis. I need to double over and hold myself
because they are so kind and keep regenerating and
recharging their kindness without any input from me.

CROW

Try to consider all three, in one, before we move in
closer. A is to B what C is to A plus B less C. Lovely.
Look again, that's right, sweep. Now left to right?
Good. Now right to left. Good. Now move across
them all for a One Two Three? Now absorb them all
at once. Now again, One Two Three? And . . . absorb.
OK, in we go:

On the left we have the dad. This image occupies the
functional position of the here-goes, the ask, what I
like to call the George-Dyer-on-the-shitter, the left-
flank, the hoist, the education spot, the empty church,
the torture step, the pain panel, the muscular.

In the middle, yours truly. A smack of black plumage
and a stench of death. Ta-daa! This is the rotten core,
the Grünewald, the nails in the hands, the needle in
the arm, the trauma, the bomb, the thing after which
we cannot ever write poems, the slammed door, the
in-principio-erat-verbum. Very What-the-fuck. Very
blood-sport. Very university historical.

But don't stop looking. The triptych is about ways
of never stopping. It is culture. On the right we have
the boys. Two forms, but one shape, could be female,
could be male, we can just about decipher four little
legs and four little arms (the newborn calf of the

right-hand panel!) and tiny little hopeful faces. And sense is suddenly made of the previous panels, this is pure mathematics, this is ancient logic. It is nature. This is what I call the lift-off, late style, the ten-year-journey-home, the arrow through the eye-hole, the fugue. Very sunset. Very bard. Very poignant.

BOYS

We all used to get a lot of trouble from
Mum for flecking the mirror with
toothpaste.

For a few years we flecked and spat and
over-brushed and our mirror was a white-
speckled mess and we all took guilty
pleasure in it.

One day Dad cleaned the mirror and we
all agreed it was excellent.

Various other things slipped. We pissed on
the seat. We never shut drawers. We did
these things to miss her, to keep wanting
her.

DAD

Oil, when you look closer mud, when you look closer sand, when you sip it, silt becoming silk.

I missed her so much that I wanted to build a hundred-foot memorial to her with my bare hands. I wanted to see her sitting in a vast stone chair in Hyde Park, enjoying her view. Everybody passing could comprehend how much I miss her. How physical my missing is. I miss her so much it is a vast golden prince, a concert hall, a thousand trees, a lake, nine thousand buses, a million cars, twenty million birds and more. The whole city is my missing her.

Eugh, said Crow, you sound like a fridge magnet.

BOYS

In the long grass I discover flattened paths,
maybe my brother's, so I whisper, 'Bro, are
you in here?' and passing adults see us,
three feet apart, but we are in cathedrals,
infinite, vast.

Crow giggles. 'I'm in here, can't see me,
I'm greeeen!'

DAD

I said to my best friend, She would be cross with
me for staying the extra day for the end-of-term
football party, because we'll hit all the holiday traffic.
My friend said, You have to stop thinking this way,
involving her. There's grief and there's impractical
obsession.

I was impractically obsessed with her before, I said.
Are you seeing anyone? he said. To talk things
through?

I am, I said.
Are they good?
Very good.

I almost laughed, at the thought of Crow in a study,
Crow pecking out an invoice, Crow recommended
by a GP, or available on the NHS. Crow pondering
Winnicott, with a shake of the head, but grudgingly
liking Klein.

Yes, I said to my best friend. You don't need to worry,
I am being helped.

BOYS

Around the time Mum died there was a hurricane and a lot of trees fell down. In the beech woods near our Gran's house there were a great many half-fallen trees, resting diagonally on the ones left standing.

I climbed up, and up, until my weight made the fallen tree slip and I would come crashing down. Sometimes into soft cushioned cradles of greenery, sometimes into nests of sharp branches. My brother would yell DEAD MEAT!

I can't remember if this game was my brother's idea, or Crow's.

Dad came to get us in the woods at dusk and said, 'You're bleeding. Fucking hell, your whole body is bleeding.' I was numb from the cold and the scratches were tingling and Dad told my brother to have a serious think about his behaviour.

CROW

This one is true:

Once upon a time there was a demon who fed on grief. The delicious aroma of raw shock and unexpected loss came wafting from the doors and windows of a widower's sad home.

Therefore the demon set about finding his way in.

One evening the babes were freshly washed and the husband was telling them tales when there was a knock on the door.

Rat-a-tat-tat. 'Open up, open up, it's me from 56. It's . . . Keith. Keith Coleridge. I need to borrow some milk.'

But the sensible father knew there was no number 56 on the quiet little street, so he did not open the door.

The next night the demon tried again.

Rat-a-tat-tat. 'Open up, open up, I'm from Parenthesis Press. It's Paul. Paul . . . Graves. I heard the news. I'm truly gutted it's taken me this long to come over. I've brought a pizza and some toys for the boys.'

But the attentive father knew there had been a Pete from Parenthesis and a Phil from Parenthesis, but never a Paul from Parenthesis, so he did not open the door.

The next night the demon ran at the door, flashing blue and crackling.

Rat-a-tat-tat. BANG. BANG. 'Open up! Police! We know you're in there, this is an emergency, you have five seconds to open the door or we will smash our way in.'

But the worldly grieving man knew a bit about the law and sensed a lie.

The demon went away and wondered what to do next. He was tabloid-despicable, so a powerful plan came to him.

Rat-a-tat-tat-tat. Knock. Knock. Knock. 'Boys? It's me. It's Mum. Darling? Are you there? Boys, open the door, it's me. I'm back. Sweetheart? Boys? Let me in.'

And the babes flung their duvets back in abandon, swung their little legs over the edge of the bed and scampered down the stairs. The chambers of their baffled baby hearts filled with yearning and they tingled, they bounded down towards before, before, before all this. The father, drunk on the voice of his beloved, raced down after them. The sound of her voice was stinging, like a moon-dragged starvation surging into every hopeless raw vacant pore, undoing, exquisite undoing.

'We are coming, Mum!'

Their friend and houseguest, who was a crow, stopped them at the door.

My loves, he said.

My dear, sorry loves. It isn't her. Go back to bed and let me deal with this. It isn't her.

The boys floated their crumpled crêpe-paper dad back up, one under each arm steering his weightlessness, and they laid him down to sleep. Then they sat at the window looking down and watching what happened and they liked it very much, for boys will be boys.

Crow went out, smiled, sniffed the air, nodded good evening and back-kicked the door shut behind him. Then Crow demonstrated to the demon what happens when a crow repels an intruder to the nest, if there are babies in that nest:

One loud KRONK, a hop, a tap on the floor, a little distracted dance, a HONK, swivel and lift, as a discus swung up but not released but driven down atomically fixed and explosive, the beak hurled down hammer-hard into the demon's skull with a crack and a spurt then smashed onwards down through bone, brain, fluid and membrane, into squirting spine, vertebra snap, vertebra crunch, vertebra nibbled and spat and one-two-three-four-five all the way down quick as a piranha, nipping, cutting, disassembling the material of the demon, splashing in blood and spinal gunk and shit and piss, unravelling innards, whipping ligaments and nerves about joyous spaghetti tangled wool hammering, clawing, ripping, snipping, slurping, burping, frankly loving the journey of hurting, hurting-hurting and for Crow it was like a lovely bin full of chip papers and ice cream and currywurst and baby robins and every nasty treat, physically invigorating like a westerly above the moor, like a bouncy castle elm in the wind, like old family pleasures of the deep species. And Crow stands thrilled in a pool of filth, patiently sweeping and toeing remains of demon into a drain-hole.

His work done, Crow struts and leaps up and down the street issuing warnings while the pyjama-clad boys clap and cheer – behind-glass-silent – from the bedroom window. Crow issues warnings to the wide city, warnings in verse, warnings in many languages, warnings with bleeding edges, warnings with humour, warnings with dance and sub-low threats and voodoo and puns and spectacular ancient ugliness.

Satisfied with his defence of the nest, Crow wanders in to find some food.

DAD

Such a bad joke, bad dream, bad poem, so different,
this cr

cr

cr

cr

cr

e ak, ik e y, evice, ea tor.

Cr

Cr

cr

y

ying

BOYS

He was young and good and sometimes
funny. He was silent then he was livid
then he was spiteful and unfamiliar, then
he became obsessed and had visions and
wrote and wrote and wrote.

Come and look at this, Crow said. Your
Dad seems to be dead!

We crept in and the room smelt of rotting
mouse and there were ashtrays in the
duvet and bottles on the floor. Dad was
spread-eagled like a broken toy and his
mouth was slack grey and collapsed like a
failed Yorkshire pudding.

Dad are you dead?
   Dad, are you dead?
   A long whining fart answered and Dad
kicked out.
   Course he's not dead, you boob, said my
brother.

60

I never said he was dead, I said.

Whoops, said Crow.

I'm not dead, said Dad.

DAD

Dear Crow,

Today I drew a picture I am really proud of. It's a picture of you, sitting on a chair, with a hand-puppet of Ted. Opposite you is Ted, sitting on a chair, with a hand-puppet of you. The likeness is superb!

Ted's hand-puppet Crow has a speech bubble. The Crow puppet is saying 'TED, YOU STINK OF A BUTCHER'S SHOP.'

I think you'd love it.

BOYS

Dad told us stories and the stories changed
when Dad changed.

I remember a story about a rat catcher.
The rat catcher nailed the tails of dead
rats to the headboard of his bed, one,
two, three, four, five. The rat catcher
killed the king of the rats and everyone
knows a king rat can't be killed unless
you boil its heart. As the rat catcher slept
the rat king's tail unpinned itself from
the headboard and went along the line
plaiting the tails of his dead fellows to
make a noose and they throttled the rat
catcher. Rat catcher, rat, said Dad, what do
you make of that?

Dad told us stories and the stories changed
when Dad changed.

I remember a story about a Japanese
writer who fell on his own sword and it

was so sharp it cut through blood and
came out clean from his back.

I remember a story about an Irish warrior
who killed his son by mistake but when he
realised he didn't mind that much because
it served the son right.

DAD

There is an area of the kitchen work surface where
I lean while the boys eat Weetabix. It is a little way
along from the area of the kitchen work surface
where my wife used to lean.

*IT IS VERY HEAVY, THERE'S NO WAY TO SAY
HOW LONG IT WILL GO ON BUT WE HAVE
GREAT FEAR FOR PEOPLE CAUGHT IN THE CITY.*

The boys hear the news. They need to know. I tell
them a lot about war.

Loss and pain in the world is unimaginable but I want
them to try.

CROW

Notes towards my voice-driven literary memoir, if I may:

I loved waiting, mid-afternoon, alone in their home, for them to come back from school. I acknowledge that I could have been accused of showing symptoms related to unfulfilled maternal fantasies, but I am a crow and we can do many things in the dark, even play at Mommy. I just pecked about, looking at this, looking at that. Lifting up the occasional sock or jigsaw piece. I used to do little squitty shits in places I knew he'd never clean.

The first thing I would hear would be the high interlinking descants and trills of chatter, sing-song and cheerfulness. The boys. There might be a thump as they smashed against the front door, then a breath-catching wait for Dad to catch up. He would open the door and with a click the flat would be full of noise, Shoes Off, Bags Down Please, Don't leave it there, I said Don't, leave it there, come on, ship chop chip shop up the stairs.

There is a beautiful lazy swagger to tired little men, they roll and flump and crash down in the interlude before beginning to scavenge for food or entertainment, and I was always filled with uncharacteristic optimism and good cheer watching them slouch unselfconsciously back into their roost. And sugar! On the evenings when he gave them treats, or they climbed up to the cupboard and plundered – crow-like – their father's stash. If you haven't observed human children after serious quantities of sugar, you must. It raises and deranges them, hilariously, for an hour or so, and then they slump.

It is uncannily like blood-drunk fox cubs.

BOYS

We collected the postman's dropped elastic
bands. We thought we would build a giant
ball. We gave up.

We made bases, camps, dens, shelters, forts,
bunkers, castles, pill-boxes, tunnels and
nests.

We watched London and London offered
us possible mothers in jeans and striped
T-shirts and Ray-Bans, so we spotted them
and liked the nasty insensitive self-harm
of it. We were blasé with a babysitter who
said, 'How can you laugh about it, it's so
sad?'

We balanced on the back of the sofa and
dive-bombed onto the carpet and Dad
shouted You think that doesn't damage
your knees but it does and when you
are my age you will have serious knee
problems OK, and I will not push you

round in a cart like sad beggars and if you
think I'm lying you should have seen
your grandmother's knees, ruined, like
an aerial shot of a battlefield, she could
hardly kneel, from childhood disrespect of
her joints, ballet, mostly, but sofa jumping
too, and they chopped her knees up, this
is before laser surgery, and if you don't
believe me you can

We stopped listening and kept on leaping.

After the advent of laser surgery but
before puberty, before self-consciousness,
before secondary school, before money,
time or gender got their teeth in. Before
language was a trap, when it was a maze.
Before Dad was a man in the last thirty
years of his life. Really, on reflection, the
best possible time to lose a mum.

DAD

'I'll tell you this for free,' said Crow.

'Hmm.' (I am trying to work, trying to entertain the notion of Crow a bit less since I read a book about psychotic delusions.)

'If your wife is a ghost, then she is not wailing in the cupboards and corners of this house, she is not mooching about bemoaning the loss of her motherhood or the bitter pain of watching you boys live without her.'

    'No?'

    'No. Trust me, I know a bit about ghosts.'

    'Go on.'

    'She'll be way back, before you. She'll be in the golden days of her childhood. Ghosts do not haunt, they regress. Just as when you need to go to sleep you think of trees or lawns, you are taking instant symbolic refuge in a ready-made iconography of early safety and satisfaction. That exact place is where ghosts go.'

I look at Crow. Tonight he is Polyphemus and has only one eye, a polished patent eight-ball.
'Go on then. Tell me.'

'Really?'

'Please.'

'I'm not a performing monkey.'

'Tell me.'

'It's more like a scent, or a synaesthetic memory, but it is something like this . . .'

He sits still. His neck ceases jutting, his beak refrains from jabbing. For the first time since his arrival he stops suggesting constant readiness for violence with his posture.

He sits as still as I have ever seen an un-stuffed animal sit. Dead still.

'Right . . . p p p, yes, ooh hold on, paradiddle parasaurolophus watch with mother spies and weddings hang on, ignore that, here we go . . .

Playdates! Red Cross building, parquet floor, plimsolls. Brownies. Angel biscuits.

Fig Rolls. Dance-offs. Fig Rolls. Patchwork for
Beginners. Invisible ink.
Chase, I mean, tag, catch, you know. Rope swings. Her
dad's massive hands.
Rock pools (Yorkshire?). Crabbing, nets, sardines,
hiding, waiting.
Counting (abacus? beads?).
Trampolines/aniseed sweets/painted eggs.
Pencil sharpenings? Magic Faraway, Robert the . . .
something, Robert the Rose Horse?'

We sit in silence and I realise I am grinning.
I recognise some of it. I believe him. I absolutely
blissfully believe him and it feels very familiar.

'Thank you Crow.'

'All part of the service.'

'Really. Thank you, Crow.'

'You're welcome. But please remember I am your
Ted's song-legend, Crow of the death-chill, please. The
God-eating, trash-licking, word-murdering, carcass-
desecrating math-bomb motherfucker, and all that.'

'He never called you a motherfucker.'

'Lucky me.'

BOYS

Once upon a time there were two boys
who purposefully misremembered things
about their father. It made them feel better
if ever they forgot things about their
mother.

There were a lot of equations and
transactions in their small family.
One boy dreamed he had murdered his
mother. He checked it wasn't true, then he
put a valuable silver serving spoon that
his father had inherited in the bin. It was
missed. He felt better.

One boy lost the treasured lunchbox
note from his mother saying 'good luck'.
He cried, alone in his room, then threw
a toy car at his father's framed Coltrane
poster. It smashed. He felt better. The
father dutifully swept up all the glass and
understood.

There were a lot of punishments and
anticipations in their small family.

DAD

The boys fight.

BOYS

The cold woke one of them, so he woke
the other saying FATHER IS GONE, and
the other agreed. Their mother had gone
– she had either lain down in the snow
and slept to death or been taken by wolves
– so they knew a thing or two about how
a small house smells and sounds when a
parent is gone, and they were right, their
father was gone.

Perhaps, said one of the boys, he'll come
back, and the other boy ruffled his hair
and smiled with his eyes, because no, he
wouldn't come back. A gone dad is a gone
dad ever.

So they sang the tidy up song as they
went about the place, putting things away,
and they put on all their clothes so they
looked much fatter than they were, and off
they went.

They walked for three days, sleeping only
as they rolled down hills, so they were
never still. They lost their childish bodies
and grew beards and popped through
layers of clothing so that by the fourth
day, when the sun came out, they were big
naked men.

Look at you, said one to the other. Look at
our willies, said the other to his brother.

They came upon a little cottage and
they knocked at the door. As soon as
the terribly beautiful woman answered
they knew they weren't ready for her
to be anything other than a mother, so
they scurried home, wee wee wee, up the
hills, across the frozen woodland, into
the house, up the stairs, into bed – eyes
squeezed shut – and when they woke up
their father was cooking breakfast.

DAD

We went to a Birds of Prey Flying Display. In a field.
Deep country somewhere, with half a dozen old dears
and the plump ginger guide with a radio mic; 'here
she comes, the star of the show.'

The first bird out was a bald eagle, stunning, massive,
with a six-foot wingspan. Ooh, yeah, we said. Ooh
yeah. The boys were transfixed.

'Now look as she decides whether or not to turn on
the OW-WOOP, THERE SHE GOES, lift, lift, UP
SHE GO GIRL, that's MY GIRL!'

And she soared. She got *lift*. We got lift.

The boys were gripping the plastic seats and the
situational artifice of the captive bird performing
dropped away and I was just excited by the bald eagle.
The physical magnificence of the eagle.

'Oh, now here you are, who's this? Oh, lordy lordy,
you tasty little bugger, excuse my language folks. It
being springtime the carrion crow in this field here
is protecting eggs, as well you would with a bloody
eagle about, HOW ABOUT THAT! That, ladies and

gentlemen, is a brave little bastard. That is a crow,
SURFIN' A BALD EAGLE!'

I turned sideways and the boys were spontaneously
holding hands.

'Ladies and gentlemen I present to you the bloody
miracle of nature. That is two birds basically giving
each other a bloody great nod of respect. You may
be many bloody kilograms heavier than me, about
forty times my size, but if you come near my eggs I'll
bloody show you a thing or two about flying!'

Up we shot, all three of us. A standing ovation.
'GO CROW!' we yelled.

'Why ever not,' said the red-faced lover of birds, our
dude, our guide, 'why ever fucken not. GO CROW!'

Go crow. Go Crow.

And that was probably the best day of my life since
she died.

BOYS

Once upon a time there was a king who
had two sons. The queen had fallen from
the attic door and bashed her skull and
because the servants in the kingdom were
busy polishing sculptures for the king,
she bled to death. The king was often
busy with futile curse-lifting and the
prevention of small wars. And so it was
that the little princes would fight.

They slapped. A little cuff, a little jab. The
short fat younger prince (called Ivan the
Lazy, or Guilty Beast, or Greedy Wolf)
would move the chair and send his brother
tumbling to the cold marble floor. Trips,
shin-kicks, tickles.

Then, as they missed their mother, more
and less, the fights got better, worse. The
handsome one (called Prince In-a-Bit, or Idle
Eagle, or Hungry Deer) would kneel on his
brother on the fleshy underarms, and roll his

knees upon the slipping muscle. They would
lie at opposite ends of the throne-room
benches and kick kick kick kick kick until his
sobbing brother pleaded mercy, harder.

Then they bit. Then they tried to drown each
other. Then they tried to burn each other's
hair. They tied each other up, they twisted
wrists, they wedgied, they spat.

Then they found a poison book and took
turns to make each other sick. Then they
hanged each other. Then they flayed each
other. Then they crucified each other. Then
they drove rusty nails into each other's skulls.

One day the king, who happened to
be strolling through the palace maze,
chanced upon his bloodied sons armed
with crossbows, each prince ablaze with
murderous intent.

'My little yearlings, my lovely hoyden boys,
why do you play this way?' asked the king.

'Because we miss our mammy so,' the little boys sang in unison.

The king roared with laughter and patted his pig-tight belly.

'My darling imps, you've got so much to learn about what it means to be king. The queen was no more your mother than she was my own. God only knows which corridor wenches spat you two out, but it certainly wasn't that friend-of-a-friend I called Queen.'

So the boys, quite relieved, shook hands and went on to become very successful kings of large and profitable kingdoms.

CROW

Krickle krackle, hop sniff and tackle, in with the bins, singing the hymns.

I lost a wife once, and once is as many times as a crow can lose a wife. Ooh, stab it. Just remembered something.

He flew a genuflection Tintagel–Carlyle cross Morecambe–Orford, wonky, trying to poison himself with forbidden berries and pretty churches, but England's litter saved him. Ley lines flung him cross-country with no time for grief, power cables catapulted loose bouquets of tar-black bone and feather and other crows rained down from the sky, a dead crow storm, a tor top burnt bird bath, but our crow picked and nibbled at Lilt cans and salted Durex and B&H, and the fire storm passed over his head, as written history over the worker. Blackberry, redcurrant, loganberry, sloe. Damson, plum-pear, crab-apple, bruises. Clots, phlegm, tumours and quince.

He looks in a puddle of oil and sees his beak is brightly coloured, striped red, green, purple and orange. Like a fucking puffin.

He opens his mouth to scream and beautiful English melody comes out, garden-song, like a blackbird or Ivor blooming Gurney.

This is another one of Crow's bad dreams.

BOYS

Once upon a time our Dad took the bus to Oxford to hear his hero Ted Hughes speak. This was when Ted Hughes was grey and nearly dead and Dad was just out of school. He'd never been to Oxford before and he was shocked that there were normal shops, McDonald's and stuff. He couldn't believe there were yobs throwing cans in the bus station. He thought there would only be professors mulling things over.

He arrived three hours too early, so he bought some records in a trendy record shop. He got something he didn't want because he was too embarrassed to correct the man behind the counter. He went to a pub and drank two pints of Guinness and smoked cigarettes, one after the other. Our Dad was quiet and shifty and romantic and you could smoke indoors then.

Our Dad was disillusioned by the size and modernity of Oxford. He had thought he might bump into Ted, or Peter Redgrove, before the reading. Then he was embarrassed at his own naïveté and had a third pint. He was reading Osip Mandelstam and underlining and folding pages, copying bits into his notebook. He had assumed the pub would be full of young thinkers behaving in the same way, but the pub was empty apart from a man in a Spurs shirt with a beagle.

Our Dad was in a shit pub right by the bus station.

He had bang-up-to-date views on Hughes and Plath. One of those views was that it was all over. It was time to shed all that crap and assess the poetry without partisan biographical bickering. He was pro-Ted, our papa. On the bus to Oxford he had imagined some vigorous arguments in a wood-panelled pub with a gaggle of Plath fans. 'OK, OK, we'll accept *River*,' they'd say. 'Fair enough,' Dad would say, 'I'll have another go at *Colossus*.'

To be fair to our Dad, he was authentic. Quiet, shifty and tragically uncool. We had to take the piss out of him as hard as we possibly could. We were convinced that it was what our Mum would have wanted. It was our best way of loving him, and thanking him.

He got a free drink with his ticket.

He kept his ticket and still has it in his Ted folder.

He sat halfway from the front.

He waited for his hero.

(Big man with a grubby marked hardback,
probably a Barbour jacket, perhaps even
the whiff of the Devon farm or a smear
of salmon guts on the pocket. The iconic
cowslip has fuzzed and faded, Dad knows,
but what will his hair be like? A smart
Laureate crew-cut perhaps. And will it all
be Shakespeare talk, or will there be a poem
or two? A new poem or two, Ted? For your
young fans? For the boys that have you up
there with Donne and Milton?)

Ted, when he did arrive, looked a little
unwell.

The talk passed by in a reverential haze. He
never remembered much of it, except that it
was very, very Shakespeare-heavy, and one
of the panel was hostile to Ted.

It was time for questions and our eighteen-
year-old Dad already had the hot neck-up
blush and sweaty palms of a question-ready
fan. At the back, a question about Caliban
and empire. Yes, Madam at the side, a
question about bad reviews. Yes, Sir, here
at the front, a question about Sylvia, met
with a sigh from the Ted-savvy crowd, and
a polite 'not relevant' from the chairperson.
Then, joy oh joy, Yes, Young Man, in the
middle.

Dad stood up, which was funny because
none of the others had. We chuckle at the
standing up.

His question was very long and very
earnest, and it came out a bit muddled, but it
was about nuclear war, and censorship, and
pollution and James the First. Ted nodded,
smiled, nodded, and the chairperson said,
'Thank you, lovely, more of an essay than
a question, but thank you. I'm sorry to say
we're out of time.'

Dad sat down painfully hard on his bum-
bones, crimson, with tears prickling.

Mum apparently cried once when he told
this story, but wait! Wait! we all shout.
Wait Dad, you tragic twat! You are not left
shamed by the chairperson! This is why we
love and mock you. There's a happy coda.

As our Dad was shuffling his way to the
exit a vast poet's hand clapped down on his
shoulder and the full-fathom-twenty drone
boom-dry loveliness of Ted Hughes' warm
Yorkish accent coated our happy Daddy.

'Yes,' said Hughes, looking Dad in the eye.
'Yes?' said our Dad.
'Yup,' said Hughes, and turned away.

And our Dad forgot what he asked, and
Ted Hughes died, and so did our Mum,
and my brother tells the Oxford story
differently to me.

PART THREE PERMISSION TO LEAVE

CROW

This is the story of how your wife died.

DAD

I've changed my mind. I don't want to hear it.

CROW

But that's the whole point. She banged her head.

DAD

Crow, really, it's fine. I know. I don't need to know.

CROW

Fancy that.

DAD

Dear Crow,

   You once stood by my bed and spoke in the voice
of black birdcall and told me never to marry again,
to seal off my heart and tie up my cock. Us crows are
monogamous, you said, and tapped my forehead with
your jut-jutting beak.

   Then, later, you stood by my bed and told me the
story of Ted. You spoke in the voice of a Yorkshire
teacher and told me to get back on it, find a lover, buck
my ideas up, think of the boys. Crack on, you said.
You should shack up with a friendly young thing who
likes the sound of 'Stepmum'. Have a roll in the hay.
I flung the duvet off and flailed and swung and spat
at you but you were elsewhere and I had to fall asleep
crushed between what you'd said and what I thought.
No sleep.

                Sharp edges.
                                Bad breath.

BOYS

Once we were doing some drawing at
the kitchen table and Dad said, 'We
can never think too much about how
important Picasso is,' and my brother said,
'Wankerama Dad!' and Dad was nearly
sick from laughing so hard.

We abused him and mocked him because it
seemed to remind him of our Mum.

Once upon a time we went to a secret
place with our Gran. It was a huge semi-
circular wall of red sand that was once in
the sea. Give it a kick and a shell would
fall out. This was in the middle of a bright
yellow rapeseed field.

Dad did not come. That was something
Dad had nothing to do with.

DAD

She had flu. It was unusual for her to be ill. The boys
were tiny and it had snowed and she couldn't bear
us rampaging about the house so we got dressed and
went sledging in the park. We were pathetic without
her. The boys didn't know where their hats were.
Couldn't get their joined mittens through their puffer
jackets; didn't want to see other boys, bigger boys
sledging on the hill. I was hopeless. I took them out
without wellies so before we'd even got down the
road their little toes were aching. They both whinged
and we all felt, the three of us, that without her things
didn't work as they should. They pitied me. I felt
acutely embarrassed that my brilliance as a father had
been exposed as wholly reliant upon her. Perhaps if I'd
known it was a dress rehearsal for the rest of our lives
I would have said BUCK UP YOU LITTLE TURDS,
or HELP ME. Or take me, take me instead please.

DAD

Things Crow is <u>NOT</u> scared of:
Ted.
Biographies of Sylvia.
God.
Wind farms.
Motherless children.
Bald eagles.
Tar Baby.
Scarecrows.
Man.
Death.

Things Crow <u>IS</u> scared of:
Divorce.
Plot.
Business.
Catholics.
Barbed wire.
Pesticides.
Gossip.
Taxidermy.
Keith Sagar.

DAD

About two years afterwards, far too soon but perfectly timed, I brought home a woman, a Plath scholar I met at a symposium.

She was funny and bright and did her best with a fucked-up situation. We had to be quiet because the boys were asleep upstairs.

She was soft and pretty and her naked body was dissimilar to my wife's and her breath smelt of melon. But we were on the sofa my wife bought, drinking wine from glasses my wife was given, beneath the painting my wife painted, in the flat where my wife died.

I haven't had sex with many women, and I only got good at it with my wife, doing things my wife liked. I didn't want to do those things, or think about whether I should be doing those things or thinking about the thinking, which meant I bashed her teeth, then knelt on her thigh, then apologised too much, then came too quickly, then tried too hard, then not hard enough.

But it was good, and she was lovely, and we sat up smoking her strong cigarettes out of the window and talking about everything we'd ever read that wasn't by or about Sylvia or Ted.

She left and I felt nervous about feeling cheerful. I walked around the flat as if I'd only just met it, long strides and over-determined checking of surfaces. I looked in on the boys.

*

When I came down Crow was on the sofa impersonating me pumping and groaning.

BOYS

We seem to take it in ten-year turns to be defined by it, sizeable chunks of cracking on, then great sink-holes of melancholy.

Same as anyone, really.

We used to think she would turn up one day and say it had all been a test.

We used to think we would both die at the same age she had.

We used to think she could see us through mirrors.

We used to think she was an undercover agent, sending Dad money, asking for updates.

We were careful to age her, never trap her. Careful to name her Granny, when Dad became Grandpa.

We hope she likes us.

DAD

Dearest boy,

One Christmas about three years after your mother died, I had put you and your brother to bed and I was sprawled on the sofa drinking red wine and reading R. S. Thomas when she walked in and said Hello. She was naked except for her socks (never a good look even when she was alive). She tripped on the rug, stumbled, and banged her knee on the coffee table. We went upstairs and I put some arnica cream on the bruise and we bickered about the mess in the medicine cupboard. Then we filled your stockings with presents and tiptoed into your rooms to lay them by your beds. I went to sleep and your mother sat up reading for a while.

That is completely true.

Are you being good? Don't worry about doing stuff or not doing stuff, it doesn't matter.

Love,

Dad

BOYS

One brother sat quietly inside the brother
bits and tried hard but felt angry. It's me.
I had a difficult few years, now I'm fine,
but I'm quiet and I'm unsentimental. My
brother calls out KRAAAA and talks to
them. The terrible years of my life were
stained crow. And here's a little secret. I've
never even read it. I don't like Hughes and
I don't like poetry.

Insanity. Pretentiousness. Denial. Indulgence.
Nonsense.

I took an air rifle into a field when I was
a teenager to shoot crows. I shot one and
wanted to keep on going. I wanted to pile
up a bonfire pile of dead black birds with
nasty beaks. But they are so clever, they
knew what I was up to and kept just far
enough away.

I went back to the one dead crow just in
time to see it limping off across the flint-
stubbled ground.

Dad had a few girlfriends but never
married again, which seemed to be the
best thing for everyone.

I'm either brother.

DAD

Moving on, as a concept, was mooted, a year or
two after, by friendly men on behalf of their well-
intentioned wives. Women who loved us. Women who
knew me as a child.

Oh, I said, we move. WE FUCKING HURTLE
THROUGH SPACE LIKE THREE MAGNIFICENT
BRAKE-FAILED BANGERS, thank you, Geoffrey,
and send my love to Jean.

Moving on, as a concept, is for stupid people, because
any sensible person knows grief is a long-term
project. I refuse to rush. The pain that is thrust upon
us let no man slow or speed or fix.

So I walked into their room in the navy blue middle
of the night in summertime and listened to them

breathing. Duvets smashed and tangled, little soft limbs emerging from robot and pirate print cotton and assorted soft toys. My wife and I used to come and tuck them in and marvel at how perfect they were asleep. We laughed at how beautiful they were – 'it's insane!' we said. It was, insane.

And I stood and breathed their air and considered – as always – things like fragility, danger, luck, imperfection, chance, being kind, being funny, being honest, eyes, hair, bones, the impossible hectic silent epidermis rejuvenating itself, never nervous, always kissable, even when scabbed, even so salty I made it, and I felt so many nights utterly, totally yanked apart by how much I loved these children, and I asked them, loudly:

Do you want to MOVE ON?

No reply.

Should we think about MOVING ON?
The swish and ruffle of air in nostrils, clacking tongues, sighs, the gentle invisible concentrated upper air of a room in the top of a flat where young people are dreaming.

No, I said, I agree, we are doing just fine.

Crow joined me as I left, shutting the door, and got me in a cosy headlock.

You're not alone, kid.

BOYS

Once upon a time I am grown up, I have a child. And a wife. And a car. I sound a bit like Dad.

We drive through the Chilterns, the Downs, the Moors, the Broads, singing *British Holidays for British People*. My Dad did that, he showed us Britain. Cader Idris, Shingle Street, Mallyan Spout. Now my tiny son shouts 'cra' when he sees a crow, because when I see a crow I shout KRAAAA.

I tell tales of our family friend, the crow.
My wife shakes her head. She thinks it's
weird that I fondly remember family
holidays with an imaginary crow, and
I remind her that it could have been
anything, could have gone any way, but
something more or less healthy happened.
We miss our Mum, we love our Dad, we
wave at crows.

It's not that weird.

DAD

'Listen-to-this, too-good-to-miss, rump-pum-pa-pum-paar-rrum.'

Parp!

'Go away Crow.'

MAN   How do you know when you've found
something worth picking at?

BIRD   Well much of it has to do with a state of
readiness, which is both instinctual (the hungers, the
vices etc.) and pragmatic (nice-looking crisp packet,
nice-looking widower). You'll remember with some
of my early work with you, that what appeared
to be primal corvid vulgarity was in fact a highly
articulated care programme, designed to respond to
the nuances of your recovery.

MAN   Did I respond as well as you'd hoped?

BIRD   Better. But the credit should go to the boys,
and to the deadline. I knew that by the time you sent
your publisher your final draft of the Crow essay my
work would be done.

MAN   I would be done grieving?

BIRD   No, not at all. You were done being hopeless.
Grieving is something you're still doing, and
something you don't need a crow for.

MAN   I agree. It changes all the time.

BIRD   Grief?

MAN   Yes.

BIRD   It is everything. It is the fabric of selfhood, and beautifully chaotic. It shares mathematical characteristics with many natural forms.

MAN   Like?

BIRD   Where to begin. Oh, feathers. Turds? Waves? Honeycomb? String? Intestines? Bones? Feathers, said that, cat-flaps, wait, no, wait, hats, maps, traps, books, rooks, creeks, peek in my beaks in my . . .

MAN   This is ridiculous.

I feel that if my wife's ghost had ever haunted me, now would be the time she'd start whispering, 'You need to ask Crow to leave.'

BOYS

This is what we know of Dad. He was a
quiet boy. He drifted off on family walks,
he doodled and drew and his feelings were
easily hurt by rough kids at school. He
didn't have a head for sums. He spent the
first twenty years of his life reading books,
being not-bad-but-not-skilled at football
and waiting for Mum. He loved the Greek
myths and Russians and Joyce. He was
waiting to be our Dad.

And then our Mum and Dad were in love
and they were truly dry-stone strong and
durable and people speak of ease and joy
and spontaneity and the fact that their two
smells became one smell, our smell. Us.

Afterwards he was quieter. He was, for two
or three years, by all accounts, very odd.
He had the perpetual look and demeanour
of someone floating, turning in the beer-
gold light of evening and being surprised

by the enduring warmth. A rolled-over
shoulder half-squint half-smile. Caught
baffled by the perplexing slow-release of
sadness for ever and ever and ever. Which
I suppose, looking back, was because of us.
He couldn't rage. He couldn't want to die.
He couldn't rail against an absence when
it was grinning, singing, freckling in the
English summer tweedle dee tweedle dum
in front of him. Perhaps if Crow taught
him anything it was a constant balancing.
For want of a less dirty word: faith.

A howling sorry which is yes which is
thank you which is onwards.

DAD

My little book on Ted Hughes did well enough. It got reviewed in the *TLS*:

'In its point-blank refusal to be constructively critical either of Hughes or his poems, it will certainly delight true fans of both.'

My scruffy Manchester-based publisher took me for lunch.

I told him my idea for a complete works of Ted Hughes annotated by Crow.

'How about a book on Basil Bunting?' he said.

I explained that Crow would violate, illustrate and pollute Ted's work. It would be a deeper, truly wild analysis, a critical reckoning and an act of vengeance. It would be a scrapbook, a collage, a graphic novel, a dissolving of the boundaries between forms because Crow is a trickster, he is ancient and post-modern, illustrator, editor, vandal . . .

'Shall we get the bill?' said my publisher. 'You have to move on. How about a little book on Piper and Betjeman?'

So I went home to talk to Crow about parting company.

I couldn't find him. I did find that the boys had flung wet balls of toilet paper onto the bathroom ceiling, which pissed me off because I'd told them that it stained the paint, and by the time I'd cleaned it up and cooked their dinner and put them to bed I realised, of course, that Crow was gone.

CROW

Permission to leave, I'm done.
Shall I final walk the loop, the Boys/Dad boundary,
hop/look/hop/stop.
Shall I final follow hunches, mourn hunt with pack
lunches?
I dreamt her arm was blue when I found her,
Red where I touched, reacted, peck-a-little, anything?
Nonsuch matte podginess gave way to bone,
Accident in the home.
She banged her head, dreamed a bit, was sick, slept,
got up and fell,
Lay down and died. A trickle of blood from an ear.
Hop/look/sniff/taste/better not. Total waste.

Lifeless cheek, lifeless shin, foot and toe. Wedding
ring. Smile.
The medics arrive, the kids at school are learning,
learning.

As you were, English widower, foliate head,
The undercliff of getting-on, groans, humps, huffs
and puffs,
Wages, exams, ball-drops, lies and ecstatic passages,
All dread dead as the wildflower meadow. Starts again
in proper time.

Some dads do this, some dads do that. Some natural
    evil, some fairly kind.
Pollarded, bollarded, was-it-ever-thus. Elastic snaps, a
    sniff and a sneeze and we're gone.
Coppiced, to grow well.

Connoisseurs, they were, of how to miss a mother.
    My absolute pleasure.

Just be good and listen to birds.

Long live imagined animals, the need, the capacity.

Just be kind and look out for your brother.

BOYS

Dad said it was high time we sprinkled
Mum's ashes.

He phoned the school in the morning
to tell them we had a sick bug. I'm in a
plague house, he joked with the secretary,
it's bad in here, they've got it both ends if
you know what I mean.

Gross. We laughed.

Out you hop kids. Coats on, hats on, let's
do it.

DAD

We went to a place she loved. I told them in the car on the way that I realised I had been an unusual dad since Mum died. They told me not to worry. I told them that all the nonsense about Crow was over, I was going to get a bit more teaching work and stop thinking about Ted Hughes.

They told me not to worry.

We parked the car and walked diagonals into the wind.

We pissed and the wind blew our wee back against our trousers.

While the boys were digging in the shingle I dozed off and when I woke up they were asleep, next to me, like guards, with their hoods up. I was warm.

I didn't wake them. I walked to the shoreline. I knelt down and opened the tin.

I said her name.

I recited 'Lovesong', a poem I like a great deal but she never thought much of. I apologised for reading it and told myself not to worry.

The ashes stirred and seemed eager so I tilted the tin and I yelled into the wind

I LOVE YOU I LOVE YOU I LOVE YOU

and up they went, the sense of a cloud, the failure of clouds, scientifically quick and visually hopeless, a murder of little burnt birds flecked against the grey sky, the grey sea, the white sun, and gone. And the boys were behind me, a tide-wall of laughter and yelling, hugging my legs, tripping and grabbing, leaping, spinning, stumbling, roaring, shrieking and the boys shouted

I LOVE YOU I LOVE YOU I LOVE YOU

and their voice was the life and song of their mother. Unfinished. Beautiful. Everything.